For all the kids, just like me, who love to dance – J.C.

For Sonny & Teddy – F.L.

First American Edition 2021
Kane Miller, A Division of EDC Publishing

Text copyright © Joseph Coelho 2021. Illustration copyright © Fiona Lumbers 2021.
The rights of Joseph Coelho and Fiona Lumbers to be identified as the author and
illustrator of this work have been asserted. First published in Great Britain in 2021
by Andersen Press Ltd.

For information contact:
Kane Miller, A Division of EDC Publishing
5402 S 122nd E Ave, Tulsa, OK 74146
www.kanemiller.com

Library of Congress Control Number: 2020949018

Printed and bound in China
1 2 3 4 5 6 7 8 9 10

ISBN: 978-1-68464-273-1

Luna Loves Dance

Joseph Coelho

Kane Miller
A DIVISION OF EDC PUBLISHING

Fiona Lumbers

Luna loves dance.
Twirling at Dad's,

leaping at Mom's.

When Luna dances
it's like the world's volume turns up,
like all colors brighten,
like sunlight sparkles behind every cloud.

Today is the day of her dance tryout.

Dance shoes – check!
Dance tutu – check!
Dance bag – check!

Mom and Dad watch as the dance teacher shows the class

a double-tap-spin
duck-dive
twirl-leap!

If Luna does well in the tryout she'll be a real dancer.
Luna is next...

Double. Tap. Spin.
Duck. Dive.
Trip! Fall!

She gets up,
takes a moment
and tries again...

Double. Tap. Spin.
Duck. Dive.
Trip. Fall.

She tries again.
Double. Tap. Spin.
Trip. Stumble. Fall!
Ouch!

Luna watches from the floor
as most of the class:
double-tap-spin, duck-dive, twirl-leap!

Watches as most of the class do well in the tryout.
Watches as most of the class become real dancers.

And it's like all sounds have been muffled,
like all colors have been dulled.
Like sunlight has been snatched away
from behind every cloud.

Mom and Dad tell her, "It's ok, not to worry.
Practice makes perfect. You can still dance."
"But I'll never be a real dancer," says Luna.

Mom takes Luna to see a musical.
Dancers leap and bound, tap and spin,
under golden lights. During the intermission
Luna shimmies to the ice cream seller.
It's like all colors are starting to glow a little.

"See, you're dancing!" says Mom.
"But I'll never be a real dancer," says Luna.

At Grandpa and Nana's house Luna plays their old jazz records and together they do dance moves called the Crazy Legs, Charleston, and Heels, strutting and laughing. It feels like all the colors are starting to sparkle a little.

"See, you're dancing," says Nana.
"But I'll never be a real dancer," says Luna.

Dad takes Luna to Carnival where she dances in the crowd to the booming bass and swirling tunes.

She does dance moves like the Rockaway and the Scooby Doo, ducking and diving, twirling and smiling.

Luna is at her cousin's birthday party.
After the candles are blown out
and the cake is eaten,
everyone plays games.

Dad lifts Luna up...

"A sun is a star when it shines,
a bell is a chime when it rings.
You're a real dancer when you dance
and your moves make colors sing."

"See, you're dancing!" says Dad.
"But I'll never be a real dancer," says Luna.

And then Grandpa puts
the music on and Luna's song
comes on and a space is cleared.
So she...

double-tap-spins,
duck-dives,
twirls and LEAPS!

Leaps like she has never leapt before
soaring high, like she is flying.

And everyone gasps and says...
"Luna you are a real dancer!"

And it's like the world's volume has been turned up, as Luna teaches her friends to shimmy.

Like all the colors are tapping their feet, as Luna shows Dad how to pirouette.

Like the sun is boogieing behind every cloud, as Luna and Mom do the Crazy Legs!

As Nana and Grandpa Rockaway and spin.
As Luna shows everyone
how to leap, leap, leap over hard times,
with joy bounding
in your heart.

Luna loves dance.